I'LL SHOW YOU CATS

by YLLA

Story by CROSBY BONSALL

Planned by CHARLES RADO
Designed by LUC BOUCHAGE

HARPER & ROW, PUBLISHERS
New York, Evanston, and London

From the tip of the nose

to the tip of the tail

a cat is very special.

I know this because

that's my nose you're looking at.

Now there are fat cats and thin cats,

old cats and young cats,

sad cats and glad cats and mad cats.

And there are smarty cats.

There are cats with stripes and cats with spots

and cats with diamonds in their eyes.

There are cats who look and cats who sit

and cats who climb and cats who fight.

And there are scaredy-cats.

If it's cats you're looking for,

if it's cats you want to know about,

if it's cats you love,

I'll show you cats.

We'll start with me.

Here I am! Here I am!
Follow me over the wall, through
the window, and under the ironing
board. Mind you don't trip on the
ironing board. I don't have to
worry, for cats never trip. Come
along and I'll show you what you
came to see....

Cats cats cats cats

You can always tell a scaredy-cat. His back is up,

his ears are flat, and his tail is thick and prickly.

But if a cat is standing tall, beware.

For he is an angry cat, and angry cats stand up and fight.

Cats' eyes are wise eyes and sharp eyes and bright eyes.
Cats' eyes can see in the dark. Did you know that?
They can see in the dark, they can see through a shadow,
they can see *you* sometimes before you see them.

Now these little cats are just opening their eyes.
They haven't seen anything—the world is so new.
They haven't seen fish swim or birds fly or mice run.

But they see their mother coming. She is coming now to carry
them away. She carries them one at a time this way because
this is the way cats carry little cats. All cats know that.

Little cats grow to be bigger cats.

And bigger cats are curious cats.

And curious cats are full of questions.

"What is this round thing?"

"Who are you?"

"When do we eat?"

"Where is my mother?"

"Why?"

"Why?"

"Why?"

"Why is a sunbeam?"

"Why does the grass grow?"

"Why can't a cat fly?"

"Why?"

"Why?"

"Why?"

Somewhere there is an answer to all the questions of a curious cat.

Maybe the answer is in this round ball.

Something is in it, for there is a glow in this round ball.

And it could be the moon
or a star
or the twinkle
of another cat's eye.

S-sh, I hear a big cat coming.

I told you I heard a big cat coming! Is it safe to come out?

Has he gone? Are you sure? If you are, I'll go on with the tour.

From the bottom of a watering can, I can see the tops of the trees.

And in one tree sits my friend the black cat.

He is listening to the wind blow

and he's watching a golden shape floating...floating.

My friend
the black cat
comes down from
the tree.
He comes closer
and closer.
He watches
and watches
that golden shape
floating.
Floating around
just a
cat's tongue away.

Here is my friend
the white cat.
He has a friend
the white mouse.
His friend
the white mouse
is not my friend the mouse.
He's the friend
of a friend
of mine.

My friend the white cat
and his friend
the white mouse
often sit and chat.
"You're much too big,"
says the mouse.
"You're much too small,"
says the cat.

"Your nails are too sharp," says the mouse. "Your tail is too long," says the cat.

"Take me as I am," says the cat. "Take me as I am," says the mouse.

My friend the white cat
gets no smaller.
His friend the white mouse
gets no bigger.
But these two friends
still sit and chat.
The small white mouse
and the big white cat.

Not all cats

have mice for friends.

Some cats have cats for friends.

One of these cats

is the friend of the other,

and the other

is a friend

of one of these cats.

And both are

friends of mine.

"I can jump higher than you,"

says one cat.

"No, you can't,

no, you can't,"

says the other.

"I'm higher," says one cat.
"I'm higher," says the other.
"No, I am, no, I am,
 NO, I AM," says one cat.

"No, I am, no, I am,
   NO, I AM,"
   says the other.
"See?"

Frankly I don't think either one of them is very high.
I, myself, am quite a jumper and I can jump higher
than those two jumpers. I can jump higher anytime. Watch.

It's just as I told you. From the tip of the nose
to the tip of the tail a cat is very special.